I Want to Drive a Fire Truck

Henry Abbot

illustrated by
Aurora Aguilera

PowerKiDS press

New York

Published in 2017 by The Rosen Publishing Group, Inc.
29 East 21st Street, New York, NY 10010

First Edition

Managing Editor: Nathalie Beullens-Maoui
Editor: Theresa Morlock
Book Design: Michael Flynn
Illustrator: Aurora Aguilera

Library of Congress Cataloging-in-Publication Data

Names: Abbot, Henry, author.
Title: I want to drive a fire truck / Henry Abbot.
Description: New York : PowerKids Press, [2017] | Series: At the wheel |
  Includes index.
Identifiers: LCCN 2016027419| ISBN 9781499426601 (pbk. book) | ISBN
  9781499426625 (6 pack) | ISBN 9781499429442 (library bound book)
Subjects: LCSH: Fire engines–Juvenile literature.
Classification: LCC TH9372 .A23 2017 | DDC 628.9/259–dc23
LC record available at https://lccn.loc.gov/2016027419

Manufactured in the United States of America

CPSIA Compliance Information: Batch #BW17PK: For Further Information contact Rosen Publishing, New York, New York at 1-800-237-9932

Contents

I want to drive a fire truck!
What would it be like?

4

Fire trucks park at the
fire station.

When the alarm goes off,
it's time to go!

Fire trucks are really big.

I have to climb stairs to get in.

I buckle my seatbelt and
blow the horn.

Let's go!

I steer the fire truck with the steering wheel. It will help us get there.

I press a button to turn on the siren. It's loud.

It tells everyone the fire truck
is on its way.

The fire truck races down the street.

With me at the wheel,
we'll get there safely.

Now we're at the fire.

I get the hose.

It's near the back of the truck.

Soon, the fire is out. Firefighters work hard to keep everyone safe.

I drive the fire truck back to the station.

It will be ready when the next fire happens.

Words to Know

hose

siren

steering wheel

Index

DATE DUE			
2019			
	FEB 7 - 2018	FEB 0 0 2018	

628.9
ABB
Abbot, Henry
I want to drive a fire truck